Why Mosquitoes Buzz in People's Ears

retold by Alison Adams

illustrated by Bill Greenhead

Visualize

Early one evening, Mosquito was flying around in the jungle when he saw his friend Iguana. "Iguana!" said Mosquito. "I just saw some yams that were as big as dinosaurs!"

"Oh please, Mosquito. No yams are that big," said Iguana.

"Oh yes they were," said Mosquito. "Come to think of it, those yams were as big as two dinosaurs! Maybe even three dinosaurs!"

"Please don't say any more, Mosquito," said Iguana. "I don't believe you. I never do. Look, I'm putting sticks in my ears so that I can't hear what you say."

"But, wait—" said Mosquito.

"I can't hear you. You should talk to someone else," said Iguana.

"Oh fine," said Mosquito. He flew away.

"Hi, Iguana," said Python to his friend.

". . . such a pest," said Iguana. Iguana still had sticks in his ears and was talking to himself about Mosquito.

"What? Am I a pest?" asked Python. Python's feelings were hurt when Iguana didn't answer. He slithered along in the grass until he saw Rabbit. "Rabbit!" he called.

But Rabbit wasn't happy to see Python. *Why is Python calling me?* Rabbit asked himself. *He must want to eat me!* He hopped away from Python as fast as he could.

When Crow saw Rabbit hopping quickly through the jungle, he thought that something was wrong. "Danger!" cried Crow. "There's danger in the jungle!"

When Monkey heard Crow's cry, he swung through the trees as fast as he could. He wanted to tell Owl about the danger so that she would be careful.

"Oh no!" said Owl. "Monkey, look what you've done! You've knocked Baby Owl out of my nest!"

"It was so dark out that I couldn't see where I was going," said Monkey.

"Well, I won't be able to hoot again until we find my baby. I'm just too sad. And the sun won't rise until I hoot, Monkey," said Owl.

"Don't worry. I'll find her for you," said Monkey. "Oh, here she is, Owl!"

Just then there was a loud roar. "I am calling a meeting," roared Lion. "RIGHT NOW!"
All of the jungle animals came running.

"It's been dark for much too long," said Lion. "Where is the sun, Owl?"

"I was too sad to hoot," said Owl. "Monkey knocked Baby Owl out of my nest and we only just found her."

"But I didn't mean to," said Monkey. "Crow was crying 'Danger!' and I wanted to tell Owl that something was wrong."

"But I only cried 'Danger!' because Rabbit was hopping so quickly," said Crow. "I thought that Rabbit was in trouble."

"But I was just trying to get away from Python," said Rabbit. "He wanted to eat me!"

"What? Rabbit, I didn't want to eat you," said Python. "I just wanted to ask you something. Iguana told me that I was a pest and I wanted to know if you agreed."

"Come to think of it, where is Iguana? He should be at this meeting," said Lion.

"I saw him by the river," said Python.

"Look, here comes Iguana now," said Monkey.

"But why does he have those sticks in his ears?" asked Owl.

"What are you all saying? I'm sorry but I can't hear you," said Iguana.

Lion walked over to Iguana and pulled the sticks out of his ears. "Python says that you called him a pest," said Lion.

"What? I never said that," said Iguana.

"Oh yes you did, when I saw you down by the river. And you didn't say anything when I asked you about it," said Python.

"I didn't say anything because I couldn't hear anything," Iguana said. "I had put sticks in my ears so I wouldn't have to hear Mosquito tell his tales. He's such a pest, that Mosquito."

"So I'm not a pest?" asked Python.

"And Python didn't want to eat me?" asked Rabbit.

"And no one was running after Rabbit?" asked Crow.

"And there wasn't any danger in the jungle?" asked Monkey.

"STOP!" roared Lion. "I know what happened. You all made something out of nothing. Each one of you thought that you knew what was going on—and you didn't."

"You're right," said Monkey. "Owl, I'm sorry for knocking Baby Owl out of your nest."

"And I'm really sorry for telling everyone that there was danger," said Crow.

"And, Python, I'm really sorry for thinking that you wanted to eat me," said Rabbit.

"And, Iguana, I'm sorry for—" Python started to say.

But then, all of a sudden, a little voice said, "Hi, everyone. What's going on? I was just down at the river and it was so low that an ant could have walked across it!"

"MOSQUITO!" roared Lion. "NO MORE! Your tales have made enough trouble in the jungle today. First, tell Iguana that you're sorry."

"Sorry, Iguana," said Mosquito. "It's just that I can't stop—"

"Oh yes you can," said Lion. "From now on, you won't be able to talk. You'll only be able to buzz. That way, you can't make too much trouble!"

Mosquito said, *"Buzz! Buzz!"*

Finally, Owl hooted and the sun came up.
And that's why mosquitoes buzz in people's ears!